# MAGGIE
# MAGPIE

# MAGGIE MAGPIE

## CATHIE BARTLAM

**Illustrated by Jacqui Thomas**

**Scripture Union**
130 City Road, London EC1V 2NJ.

By the same author:
**Operation Sandy** – Tiger Book
**Tricky Business** – Tiger Book
**Go for Gold** – Leopard Book
**Stranded!** – Leopard Book

© Cathie Bartlam 1991
First published 1991

ISBN 0 86201 687 8

Phototypeset by Input Typesetting Ltd, London
Printed and bound in Great Britain by Cox and Wyman
Ltd, Reading

# Chapter One

Lynsey and Paul were having lots of fun in the park. It was a huge open piece of land. There were woods and big stretches of grass. Best of all was a stream, that gurgled its way through the park.

As soon as they had left the car, Lynsey and Paul had run to the stream. It was a very hot day, but the sparkling shallow water felt very cold. While Mum watched, they paddled. Then they tried to build a dam. The stones were heavy and slippery and made big splashes when Paul put them next to each other. He was big and strong but then he was nine, a year and a half older than Lynsey. Lynsey was fast and full of ideas. She wished she could carry the big stones. Instead she told her brother where to put them.

Slowly a pool of water grew behind the dam. They stood in it, feeling it tickle their knees.

Paul decided to swim in the cool water. He forgot to tell Mum first. He also forgot to take his clothes off. Mum was a bit cross, but she laughed as well. She had some spare clothes and afterwards she made them both play somewhere else.

Dad played catch with them, then they all played cricket. Lynsey thought the bat was hard to hold. She still hit the ball though, until Paul caught her out. After Dad's turn, Mum was in for ages.

'Come on Mum. Let me have a turn.' Paul was fed up with bowling the ball. Mum kept hitting it for miles. Lynsey was puffed out running to fetch it.

'One more go,' Mum was enjoying herself. 'Then we'll have our picnic.'

Dad was unpacking the picnic box. Lynsey loved picnics. She could eat what she wanted. No one told her to finish her vegetables or to slow down. She took a chunk of cheese, crisps and a banana, and sat on the short scratchy grass. Her pale legs were going gold in the sun. Her fair hair was even blonder, but not as much as Paul's. His hair was nearly white.

'Let's go for a walk in the woods,' said Mum. 'I'll put the stuff back in the car. Then we can get out of this hot sun.'

The woods were dark and shadowy. The

path was covered in pine tree needles and felt springy to walk on. All of a sudden, they came to a grassy bit, where the sunlight danced through the gap in the trees.

'Look! Someone's lost a ball!' Paul ran to fetch it.

But it was not a ball. It was fluffy, black and white. They all crouched round it. Two tiny eyes looked at them.

'What is it?'

'A baby magpie, Lynsey.'

'Well what is it doing here?'

'I don't know,' said Mum. 'Perhaps it is waiting for its parents.'

'Where are they?'

'I don't know. We'll sit over there, very quietly, and see if they come back.'

They sat and sat. The baby waddled near to them.

'I know,' said Dad. 'We'll take her to the nature centre. Someone there will know what to do.'

He wrapped the bird in a handkerchief and carefully lifted her in his hands. Lynsey gently stroked the tiny head; the downy feathers felt like fur. The bird was not scared at all.

Dad showed the bird to the man working at the nature centre.

'Must have fallen out of her nest,' he said.

'Can you put her back?' Lynsey asked.

The man smiled. 'No. Best thing is to take her back to the wood. Magpies are a real nuisance. A fox or cat will take care of her.'

'He means kill her,' Paul said.

'But you can't!' Lynsey was nearly crying. 'Don't let them kill her. Please. Can't we take her home?'

'I don't think so,' said Mum. 'Better take her back to the wood.' But Mum looked sad as well.

'Mum, *please*. I'll look after her.'

'Lynsey, the baby bird is hurt. She has got something wrong with her neck. She might not get better.' Mum was bending down by her.

'She will! I know she will. Please?'

At last Mum and Dad gave in. Paul made a nest in one of the sandwich boxes. He tried to give the bird a piece of bread but she was not hungry.

Lynsey did not want to play any more. She sat holding the bird in the box.

'I'm going to call you Maggie Magpie,' she said. 'You're mine now. Okay?' Lynsey was sure Maggie could understand. 'You can come to live at my house. We'll be friends.'

When it was time to go home, Lynsey sat in the back of the car. She held the box very carefully. Dad was told to drive slowly so

Maggie would not get bumped. At last they reached home. Lynsey was excited. Her own baby bird to look after!

# Chapter Two

As soon as they got home, Dad found an old cardboard box. Lynsey helped him rip up some newspaper and they made a soft bed for Maggie.

'Hey look!' said Paul, 'Her neck's all wrong.' He pointed to a sore bit where the bone was sticking out. It was horrible.

'She'll be all right,' said Mum, but Lynsey did not think she meant it.

'Let's see if she'll eat something,' Mum said. She got some tiny bits of cheese, but Maggie was not interested. They tried bread, cornflakes, corned beef, grapes, a cold sausage. But nothing worked.

'We'll leave it for now,' said Mum. 'She's tired,' and she put the bird into her box.

Lynsey was tired as well. After some beans on toast for supper, she went to bed. When Dad came up to say goodnight, Lynsey was still sitting up. Usually she would be snuggled under the duvet with her toy pony on one side, and her baby doll on the other. Tonight the toy pony was still on the floor.

Dad sat on the bed and ruffled Lynsey's hair.

'Dad?'

'Yes, Lynsey?'

'Dad, what will happen to Maggie? She'll die if she can't eat, won't she?'

'I'm not sure. Why don't we talk to God about her? He cares for everybody. There's even a bit in the Bible about God knowing what happens to the sparrows.'

'But Maggie's not a sparrow!'

'Well, I'm sure God cares for magpies as well. Shall we pray?'

'Okay.' Lynsey shut her eyes really tight, to let God know this prayer was special.

'Thank you, God, for a nice day. Please help Maggie. Please make her eat something. Please make her neck better. And please don't let her die. Amen.'

Dad also talked to God. Lynsey fell asleep thinking about the little black and white ball of feathers in the box in the kitchen.

The next morning Maggie was alive. She would not eat anything but had made a smelly mess in the box. Mum said that her insides were working.

'She's got to get used to us,' said Mum. 'Here, put her on the window ledge to watch us. I'll wash and you can help dry up.'

'She'll scratch me,' said Lynsey.

'Try it.'

Very carefully Lynsey put her hands round Maggie. The bird was not afraid at all. She was so light that Lynsey could hardly feel her. Her claws did not scratch. They were soft, like finger nails when you have been playing in the bath for a long time.

Maggie looked so funny watching them. She liked the noise of the water and tried to walk along the window ledge. Her legs were thinner than matchsticks and kept going different ways. Her wings were so small, they were hardly there. She had just two feathers where Mum said her tail would grow.

Lynsey did not want to go to school, but Mum said she would look after Maggie. Mrs Henderson, Lynsey's teacher, said she could bring the bird to school.

After school Mum met Lynsey at the gates. Mum was excited.

'She's eating,' said Mum.

'Eating?'

'Yes, Maggie is eating. I'll show you as soon as we get in.'

Lynsey got Maggie out of her box. Mum did

not tell her to hang up her anorak, or put her bag away as usual.

'You hold her, Lynsey . . . now watch.'

Maggie just fitted into her hands, with her head poking out by Lynsey's thumbs.

Mum got some grey smelly mush, shaped like a tiny worm. Maggie opened her mouth wide and made a noise like a kitten. Mum put some of the food on her finger and pushed it right down Maggie's red mouth. Down and down, until Lynsey could hardly see it. The bird gave a gulp and the food was gone. Well, most of it. Some was stuck onto her feathers, and some on Mum and Lynsey.

'Now you try, Lynsey.'

'But I'll hurt her . . . and it stinks.'

'You won't. It's only minced meat soaked in milk.'

Lynsey had a go. It felt really strange pushing the stuff down Maggie's throat. If someone did that to me, thought Lynsey, I would be sick! Maggie was soon full up.

'Right, take her to play, while I get some work done. If she makes a mess, wipe it up with this.' Mum gave Lynsey a cloth that smelt like the school toilets just after they had been cleaned.

'Mum, can I take her to school tomorrow?'

'No, Lynsey. That's not a good idea.'

'But why, Mum?'

'Maggie's too little. She'll be frightened and might get hurt.'

'Mrs Henderson said I could.' If Lynsey's teacher said it was all right, then why was Mum making a fuss?

'I'll explain to her tomorrow. She probably didn't realise how little Maggie is. No arguing.'

Paul came into the kitchen and scooped up the bird. He and Lynsey took her into the garden to play. They sat on the back step, carefully holding Maggie.

'She'll be all right now, won't she, Paul?' Lynsey wanted Paul to tell her everything was all right.

'I expect so. We can take turns to look after her.' The doorbell rang. 'It's your turn. That'll be Mark to play football,' and Lynsey was left happily holding Maggie Magpie.

# Chapter Three

Every day after school Lynsey played with Maggie. She was slowly getting stronger. As soon as she saw Lynsey, she would make a funny squawk. Lynsey would pick her up and take her to have a game.

One of Maggie's favourite games was in the living room. Lynsey would throw some shiny milk-bottle tops onto the floor. Maggie would peck at them and try to pick them up with her beak. If she got excited, her short stubby wings would flap wildly.

When the television was on, Maggie would sit on the floor watching it. Then she would jump on to the low shelf by the television. Her sharp beak tapped at the moving pictures. She could not understand what they were, or where they had gone.

Then one day Lynsey came home from school with a headache. For the next week she was quite poorly and had to lie down on the settee or in bed. She got fed up watching television and did not want to read.

'Mum, I'm bored,' Lynsey called from her room.

'I've got an idea.' Mum came into the room carrying Maggie's box. 'I must be mad but I'll let you have Maggie in here for a bit.'

Lynsey and Maggie had a great time. Lynsey soon forgot to be bored. She built Lego models for Maggie to climb over. She kept finding her when Maggie explored under the bed. They played marbles together. Maggie chased the shiny glass balls across the carpet. Perhaps the nicest times were when they were both tired. Lynsey lay in bed and made a hollow in her soft duvet. Maggie would lie in the hollow while Lynsey gently stroked her, with just one finger.

The only problem was Maggie's mess. She plopped all over the bedroom and Mum kept on cleaning it up. When Lynsey was better she had to clean it up herself.

'You're my friend,' said Lynsey. She loved Maggie very much. Paul, Mum and Dad all *liked* her, but only Lynsey *loved* her.

When Lynsey was nearly better, Mum kept fussing.

'You've got to wear your slippers.'

Lynsey hated them. They looked stupid with

shorts and baggy T-shirts. Maggie, however, loved them. If Lynsey kept still, Maggie would climb onto the slippers. There she would pull bits of fluff off. Then she would fall asleep, curled up on Lynsey's foot.

As she got bigger, Maggie would go for rides on the slippers. Lynsey had to walk around the room with her legs very straight. Maggie clung on, making her funny noises and trying to stand up properly for her ride. They looked very funny, walking around together.

One day after Lynsey had gone back to school, Mum came into the classroom. Lynsey was surprised.

'Quiet children,' called Mrs Henderson. 'Lynsey's mum has kindly brought something to show us all. You must be quiet or you'll frighten her.'

'It's Maggie!' shouted Lynsey.

'That's right. It's Lynsey's baby magpie.'

Mum took her out of the box and all the children watched as Maggie walked up and down Mrs Henderson's desk. They laughed when she knocked some pencils over. And again when Maggie pecked the silvery scissors. After ten minutes, Mum put her back into the box.

'Thank you.' Mrs Henderson said goodbye to Mum and then turned to the class. 'I want us all to draw some pictures of birds. They can be magpies, like Maggie. Or any sort. I've got a pile of books here to give you ideas.'

Lynsey spent all the rest of the afternoon drawing Maggie. She coloured her playing marbles. She felt really happy. All her friends had seen Maggie, and the teacher liked her picture. In fact it was going on the wall with some of the others.

After school Mum took Paul and Lynsey shopping. Tonight Aunty Chris, Uncle Vic, and their cousins Rebekah and Jonathan were coming to stay. They were all going to squash in the house for the night.

Lynsey helped Mum choose their favourite foods. Chocolate ice-cream, crisps, cakes, yoghurts and blackcurrant jam. When they got home, they got the beds ready. Rebekah was eight, just a few months older than Lynsey, and she would share her bed. Jonathan was having a blow-up lilo in Paul's room. He was six but very adventurous and liked copying his older cousin. Mum and Dad were camping out in the living room so Aunty Chris and Uncle Vic could have their bed.

It took ages to get ready, and at last everybody arrived, hot and tired out. After a big supper, all the children were sent up to bed. But not to sleep. The four of them crept into

Lynsey's room. Paul smuggled Maggie out of the garage where she slept, and they all played with her.

Rebekah had long straight brown hair and Maggie loved it. She kept on picking up bits of it in her beak and trying to walk away with it. Jonathan tried to make her do it to his. Paul put Maggie on his cousin's head. Jonathan's hair was so slippery she skidded off.

All the laughs brought Dad upstairs. He had thought they were asleep. He removed Maggie and got them all in their right rooms. There they whispered and giggled for ages, until sleep finally claimed them.

# Chapter Four

Lynsey woke up and found that her head was where her feet should be. Next to her were her cousin's toes. She tickled them and Rebekah woke up.

'I'm starving,' said Lynsey. 'Let's make breakfast.'

They crept downstairs to the kitchen, and each got a big bowl of cereal. Lynsey made some tea. She got a bit confused and put three tea-bags in the kettle. At least it turned the water brown, and when they added lots of milk it tasted fine.

'We're going to Gunner's Wood,' Lynsey stated.

'Gunner's Wood?'

'It's ace, Rebekah. There's this big adventure playground and woods and hills and trees to climb.'

'I wish the others would hurry up so we can

go!'

Mum and Aunty Chris took hours to make a picnic.

'Lynsey, don't forget to feed Maggie!' called Mum.

'I won't.' But in all the hustle, Lynsey forgot her baby bird. Maggie's box was in the garage, away from all the noise.

Gunner's Wood was brill! Dad and Uncle Vic kept climbing up the rope ladders and Aunty Chris loved the slide. Lynsey tried to stop Mum swinging on the old tyres, but it was no use. Lynsey was not sure what she thought about grown-ups playing like children.

'Look at us!' Paul was sitting on top of a tree-house roof. Even worse, so was Jonathan. He was half Paul's size yet climbed everywhere.

'Get down,' yelled Uncle Vic, hanging upside down, red faced, from his ladder.

'Can't.'

'Well stay up there, then!' He turned to Lynsey's dad. 'I'll get that boy to obey me, one way or another!'

In the end Paul lowered Jonathan from the roof and scrambled down himself.

'I'm ready for a coffee, Sis,' called Uncle Vic.

'Don't call me Sis,' shouted Mum, unearthing a huge flask, 'I'm not eight now.'

'Act like it though,' replied Uncle Vic, as the

grown ups sat at a picnic table laughing and joking.

'Just stay in the playground,' called Dad. But by now the children wanted to explore a bit further.

'What's over there?' asked Rebekah, pointing to an interesting path that led into the woods.

'Let's find out,' said Paul.

'But Dad said to stay here,' Lynsey looked worried.

'It's all right. We can hear them. Uncle Vic must be telling funny stories again, judging by the noise they're making.' Paul was right.

The four found a stick each and set off.

'Just a little way,' said Jonathan, walking through the thick bushes rather than on the path.

The little way became a longer way. Rebekah and Lynsey picked flowers while the boys swished their sticks through the undergrowth.

The path was joined by others and then divided.

'Look, we'll just go to the water,' called Paul.

They all ran to what they thought was a pool. But it was a huge puddle in a brown hollow. Lynsey and Jonathan were racing each other. They were running so fast they could not stop.

Splash! Splurge! Straight into the puddle. Mud squelched over their trainers, past their socks. It felt wonderful. Squishy! squashy! slurpy! ploppy!

'Get out!' said Paul. As the oldest, he realised Mum would have a fit.

'In a minute,' Jonathan's cheeky face was covered with a grin, along with splashes of mud.

'You're all dirty,' Rebekah said, as her brother carried on, 'like a hippo in a mud bath.'

'Stop fussing. Come on, Lynsey, we'd better get out.'

But Lynsey had stopped laughing. She'd stopped splashing.

'I can't get out.'

'Course you can,' Jonathan splodged over to her and pulled her arm. He went straight over on his backside.

'I'm stuck!'

It was true. Lynsey was nearly crying. Jonathan's trainers had come off and were slowly sinking into the mud.

'Paul! Rebekah! Do something!'

Paul got a long stick but could not reach the trapped pair. He started to wade into the puddle but stopped. That would only make him stuck too.

'We'll shout.'

Even four voices soon got lost in the woods.

'We're lost,' said Rebekah. 'Where's Mum?'

'Look, shout some more.' But it was no

good. No one could hear them, and Lynsey and Jonathan were very scared.

'Let's talk to God,' said Paul. 'He'll sort it out.'

'Please, Jesus, will you help us to get out of the puddle?'

'And find Mum and Dad.'

'And find my new trainers,' added Jonathan.

'Sorry for going wandering off,' finished Paul.

They stood there waiting. Every few minutes they yelled 'Help' as loud as they could.

Would anyone help them? Lynsey and Jonathan wondered if they would spend the rest of their lives stuck in a muddy puddle.

# Chapter Five

Every minute seemed to last for ages. Paul could stand it no longer.

'I'll go and find Mum and Dad. Rebekah, stay here with these two.' Paul set off along the path which he thought led back towards the adventure playground.

Suddenly Lynsey and the others heard a thrashing, bashing noise in the bushes. A big brown and white dog bounded up to them. His long pink tongue flicked from side to side as he tried to lick Rebekah.

'Gerroff,' she cried.

'Gregory! Gregory! Here, boy!' a voice called.

Gregory? What a weird name for a dog, thought Lynsey.

A middle-aged man, wearing a blue T-shirt, brown trousers and green wellies strode into the clearing.

'It's all right,' he called to Rebekah, who was trying to get away from the friendly furry mat. 'Down! Gregory, down!'

'They're stuck.' Rebekah pointed. 'In the mud, and Paul's gone and Mum only got Jonathan's trainers yesterday and we can't find them.'

The man looked at the puddle and saw what the problem was.

A woman joined him. 'Arthur, what is going on?'

'They're stuck. Good job I always wear my boots in the woods.'

The man, Arthur, waded into the mud and pulled Lynsey out. Then he went back and scooped up Jonathan. He got smelly mud all over his clothes.

'My trainers!' called Jonathan. He was not bothered about anything else.

Arthur poked around with his stick and found them. Thick gooey mud poured out of them. You would have never known that they were once white. Jonathan put them back on.

'Now then,' said the woman, 'where are your mummies and daddies?'

'Mum and Dad,' corrected Lynsey. She had long stopped calling them mummy and daddy. 'They are in the adventure playground.'

'Up the rope ladder,' said Jonathan.

'My, you have wandered a long way. Come on, Arthur, let's return these poor little mites to their frantic parents.'

The 'poor little mites' had recovered very well. They felt happy at being rescued, but Rebekah was worried.

'They'll go mad when they see you. All the mud.'

'Mum is used to it,' said Lynsey. 'I always get in a mess.' She was quite proud of the fact.

'Paul! Rebekah!' The voice of one of the parents came through the wood.

'We're here,' the three children chorused, while Gregory barked loudly.

Uncle Vic came into sight.

'Where have you been? What on earth . . .? Jonathan! Your *feet*!'

Jonathan smiled and kept quiet. Everyone else talked at the same time.

'We found them stuck.'

'Gregory found them.'

'It was Lynsey's fault.'

'Wasn't, then!'

'Was.'

'. . . so I said to Arthur, we'd better find their parents.'

Uncle Vic managed to piece together what had happened. He thanked Arthur and his wife and quickly set off along the path with the children.

'Come on, back to base,' he said. 'Everyone is searching for you, except your mum, Lynsey. She has stayed at the playground. Hurry up.'

They hurried up and soon met the rest of the family. Aunty Chris got very annoyed about the mud. Lynsey's mum told them off, hugged them and burst into tears. Dad gave them a lecture about wandering off and Uncle Vic found a packet of biscuits, which made everyone feel better.

'We asked Jesus to help someone find us,' said Lynsey.

'So did we,' said Dad. 'I'll just say thank you to him.' He paused. 'Where's Paul?'

'He came to find you,' Rebekah told him.

But Paul had not found them. He kept walking the wrong way and he was very scared. He talked out loud to himself. 'Be back soon, must be this way. I'm lost. Please help me. I'm lost.'

He was very surprised when he found himself back at the muddy puddle. No sister. No cousins. Paul sat down and sniffed back the tears. He would be lost here forever. And the others had been found! It was not fair!

'Paul! Paul!'

'Here!' He jumped to his feet. 'Dad.' Paul ran to him words tumbling from his mouth. 'It wasn't my fault. I tried to find you. I've walked miles.'

Dad caught Paul in his arms. 'It's okay. No one is blaming you. We're just glad to find you.'

'Me, too,' replied Paul. Then he let his dad lead him to the others. They were all happy to see him. Straight away they tucked into their picnic, which helped them to recover from the adventure.

# Chapter Six

As soon as they had eaten, the grown-ups said that they all had to go back home and get cleaned up.

'We're all right,' said Jonathan. He was quite used to the dried mud stuck all over him.

'Home. You are filthy,' insisted Lynsey's mum. So that was that. Jonathan's clothes were taken off. He was wrapped in a green travel rug and went charging round the car park whooping like a Red Indian. His dad caught him and when they got back to Lynsey's house, Jonathan was the first to go into the shower.

Lynsey and Rebekah had a shower together. Then they sat in the bath and let the bubbly water come right up their bodies.

'Were you scared?' asked Rebekah, as she splashed the bubbles to make them bigger.

'A bit,' Lynsey admitted. 'I didn't like being stuck.'

'I didn't like being lost,' said Rebekah.

'Well I was lost *and* stuck,' replied her cousin.

'What would have happened if Arthur and his wife hadn't found us?'

'I don't know.' They were both silent, floating toy farm animals, on the bath water.

'Do you think I'd have been stuck for ever?' Lynsey's blue eyes looked enormous as she looked at Rebekah.

'No, not forever. Perhaps for a week, or a year.'

'A year! Then we'd miss summer holidays, and Christmas and my next birthday and . . .'

'Well, perhaps not a year. Anyway, Lynsey, we asked Jesus to find us. He wouldn't have left us for long. Dad says Jesus knows how we feel.'

'He must know I was scared then,' said Lynsey. She felt glad and safe. Jesus knew how she felt in the woods. He had not let her stay scared for very long.

The water was going cold. The two girls dried themselves in soft towels and went downstairs to play.

'You lot,' called Lynsey's mum. 'Play in the back garden, not out the front. I don't want any more adventures today.'

At teatime Jonathan and Lynsey went with Uncle Vic to fetch some fish and chips. Mum

had only just finished getting thick mud off their clothes and had thrown the dirty clothes into the washing machine.

In the chip shop, they held up the queue for ages, while they decided what to buy. Three fish, a battered sausage, four different pies, and a mountain of chips later, they got back into the car. All the smells got mixed up together, and the hot food packages made sweaty red marks on Jonathan's and Lynsey's legs.

After tea, when they were so full, there was only room for chocolate ice-cream, the children all watched television. They lay in a row on their tummies, gazing at the cartoons. They looked like a heap of puppies sprawled across the floor.

Very soon it was time for the cousins to go. Lynsey was tired and felt like crying. They had had such a good time together and now it was over.

'Our turn to visit you next,' Mum said as she gave Uncle Vic a hug. 'Just don't take us to any muddy woods.'

'Okay, Sis,'

'I told you, no more Sis!'

As they drove away Mum turned to Lynsey, 'Bed, I think.'

'Oh, Mum.'

'Come on, bed. It's been a lovely long day.'

Lynsey snuggled down, waiting for Dad to come upstairs. He looked more tired than she felt. He started to read her a story, but she was not listening. Her mind was going back over the day. Suddenly she remembered something.

'Dad,' Lynsey tried to climb out of bed. 'It's Maggie! I forgot all about her. I haven't fed her or changed her straw.'

'Calm down. It's okay. I've fed her, and I took her into the back garden while you were at the chip shop. She's fine.'

'Are you sure?' asked Lynsey.

'Course I am. Mind you, it's a good job there is not just you to look after her. We all can help.'

'But she's *mine*.'

'Well, sort of. But we can all help. You see, Lynsey, we all need help sometimes.'

'Like you feeding Maggie.'

'Yes,' said Dad, 'Or Arthur and his wife getting you all out of the mud.'

Lynsey was getting the idea. 'And you and Uncle Vic hunting for Paul.'

'And even the chip shop helped. Got us our tea.' Dad carried on. 'God made us to need other people. We could thank him for the different ones who have helped us today.'

Lynsey shut her eyes. 'Thank you God, for Arthur and his wife and the dog with the funny name . . .'

'Gregory,' said Dad.

'Gregory, and Uncle Vic and Aunty Chris. And Rebekah and Jonathan to play with, and Dad 'cos he didn't forget Maggie, and the chip shop lady for my battered sausage.' Lynsey paused to think. 'And people who make cars so we can go to Gunner's Wood and Mum for getting us clean and even Paul.' Lynsey could not quite think what to say about Paul so she finished with a loud 'Amen.'

As she drifted off to sleep, she said one last prayer. 'And thank you for me, and adventures, and that Maggie needs me.'

# Chapter Seven

Over the next few days Lynsey found that
Maggie needed her a lot. Mostly to stop her
getting into trouble.

Maggie could not fly but she ran fast. She
could jump quite high and kept finding herself
in all sorts of places. Mum left the cupboard
door open and Maggie discovered all the cereal
boxes. Another time she pecked away at the
pans. When one of the lids toppled off, the
noise made her run away. It did not stop her
from creeping up on the shining steel pans
whenever she had the chance.

The worst trouble was the cherries. Paul
loved cherries and Mum kept on buying them.
After school he sat in the back garden with
Lynsey. They were having a competition to see
who could spit the stones the farthest. It was
good fun. Maggie kept chasing the stones. Perhaps she thought it was like the marbles game.

Anyway, as she pecked at a stone, she got a taste of the cherry. That was it. She loved it.

Mum was gardening, trying to ignore the flying cherry stones.

'Whatever you do,' she called, brushing back her hair with a muddy hand, 'don't feed that bird with those cherries.'

'But she likes them.'

'They won't do her any good,' said Mum.

While Mum went off to have a wash and get changed, Paul and Maggie disappeared.

'Lynsey,' a loud whisper from the garage showed where they had gone. 'Come and look.'

In a secret dark corner of the garage, Paul was feeding bits of cherry to Maggie. Her neck was stretched as high as she could make it. Her mouth was open wide and only closed for a split second to gulp down the sweet fruit.

Dark red juice, like blood, dripped down her front. It also dripped off Paul's hands. When all the cherries had gone Maggie looked for some more. Lynsey was sure her fluffy tummy was much bigger.

'Clean her up,' said Lynsey. They tried to rub the red juice off Maggie, but she hated the cold water, so they left her alone. Maggie was so full up she fell asleep on the garage floor.

'I don't know why Mum made such a fuss,'

said Paul, safely putting the bird in the box. 'Maggie loved the cherries.'

Later, after tea, Paul and Lynsey found out why Mum had made a fuss.

Maggie had woken up and, as usual, gone to explore downstairs while the family had tea. As it was hot, they had eaten in the garden. When Mum went back into the house she shrieked, 'Come and see what Maggie has done!'

Maggie had gone from the garage, through the dining room, round the kitchen and into the cereal cupboard. Then she went down the hall, into the living room and onto the shelf under the coffee table.

Everywhere she had been there was purple bird plop. Masses of it all over the place. Paul thought it was very funny and could not stop laughing. The more he laughed, the more mad Mum got.

'You fed that bird cherries, didn't you?' she cried.

There was no point in saying he had not. The evidence was all over the place. Paul and Lynsey had to help clean up the mess. Purple plop makes a terrible mess and some stains never came out of the carpet.

From then on Maggie was banned from the living room. So were Paul and Lynsey, until

Maggie stopped making purple plop.

Lynsey did not mind the ban too much. She was busy teaching Maggie to do things.

Learning to perch and balance on a twig was easy. Maggie fell off only a few times. At first she would balance on Lynsey's hand, then her finger and then on a little twig.

One day Mum shouted, 'Put her in the tree.'

Lynsey placed her in the old apple tree. Maggie looked around and wobbled a lot.

Every afternoon, after school, Lynsey would take her down the garden and put her in the tree. Maggie learned to hop around the branches but she still needed Lynsey to get her back down. Lynsey would sit on a thick branch by the bird, watching her. Sometimes she would stroke Maggie's growing feathers.

Lynsey wondered what it would be like to be a bird. It would be fun to hop around tree branches, and to fly. If Lynsey could fly she would be able to see her house from the sky, and school, and her friends. And even where Rebekah and Jonathan lived. She could float around all day long.

She stretched out her arms. Now they were wings. She flapped them up and down and jumped out of the tree. Arms were no good for flying, thought Lynsey. She had landed in a heap in the rhubarb. Maggie, disturbed by the flying girl, landed next to her.

Lynsey ran up the garden and called 'Maggie!' The bird ran towards her. She squawked loudly and flapped her funny wings. Then Lynsey hid behind the shed.

'Maggie, find me,' and Maggie set off looking for her friend. Lynsey thought she looked like someone shopping in the supermarket. One of those people in a rush. The sort who nearly run and bash their shopping trolley into you. Maggie could run so fast and always squawked when she found Lynsey. It was a strange game of hide and seek but they both enjoyed it.

# Chapter Eight

One morning Maggie decided to play another game of hide and seek.

At night she slept in her box in the garage. Lynsey covered the box with an old tea-towel and asked God to look after her. Then in the morning, before breakfast, Lynsey would remove the towel and feed her.

One morning she was not in the box. Lynsey called 'Maggie!' lots of times but she did not come. All the family looked for her. At last they found her fast asleep in a gap between the wall and a pile of wood.

'Right,' said Dad. 'If she can get out of her box, she can learn to fly.'

He scooped Maggie up and went out into the garden. Everyone followed and watched.

Dad held her firmly and threw her. Just *threw* her into the air! Maggie sort of spluttered and landed on the grass. She squawked angrily.

Lynsey was cross. 'Dad, stop it. You'll hurt her.'

'I won't, Lynsey. Maggie has got to learn.' And he caught the bird who had crawled into a bush. Then he threw her into the air again.

Maggie showed no signs of even trying to fly so they gave up. Lynsey was angry. She wondered how Dad would have felt if he had been woken up, taken outside and thrown into the air. Lynsey shared her bowl of cereal with Maggie. The bird sat on her foot during breakfast. The pink slippers got quite sticky with milk and cornflakes.

'Dad, don't do it again,' Lynsey said.

'Lynsey, she's *got* to learn to fly. She has got to learn to feed herself. Or she'll never go back to the wild.'

Lynsey was quiet. Never go back to the wild! Lynsey did not want Maggie to go anywhere, ever. Maggie's home was here, with her. She could live in the garage forever. Or if she did not like that, she could live in the garden. Lynsey wanted Maggie to learn to fly. But not yet. Not until Lynsey could make sure she would not fly away.

'Lynsey,' Dad said gently. 'Maggie belongs to the wild. She does not belong here. She's got to learn.'

From then on Mum and Dad were always

saying 'she's got to learn'. They gave the flying lessons a rest. Maggie just was not ready.

Maggie would stand on the grass and stretch her long thin black legs. Her knees were really knobbly. She tried to spread her wing feathers at the same time. At first she was hopeless and would fall over. As she got more clever, she would take one wing feather at a time and run it through her beak. No-one taught her how to do it. She just knew. Mum said it was because God made her like that.

As her tail feathers started to grow, she did the same with them. All her feathers were growing very quickly. Paul tried to measure them but Maggie did not like that idea. She ran away whenever Paul got near her with a ruler.

Lynsey used to sit and watch her for hours. Marie, her friend, would come to play. As the two girls sat on the grass, Maggie would climb and hop onto them. She liked to sit on their shoulders. There she could play with their hair. Sometimes she jumped onto Lynsey's head. Together they would go for a walk round the garden, the bird balancing on Lynsey's head.

Lynsey pretended that she was an old ship's captain with a parrot on her shoulder. She would limp and shut one eye. That was because captains always had a wooden leg and an eye patch in story books. 'What ho! my hearties,

land ahoy!' Paul said she was nuts but Lynsey ignored him. She could pretend to be whoever she wanted to be. Maggie, however, refused to talk and never learned to say, 'Pretty Maggie.'

Marie and Lynsey had competitions. They had to see who could walk the farthest before Maggie fell off their head or shoulder.

It did not hurt Maggie to fall now. She would stick her wings out and flutter onto the ground. She was getting cheeky. If Lynsey put her biscuit down, Maggie would grab it. Running down the garden, she would try to eat it. She was much better at stealing food than at eating it. So, after a bit Lynsey would pick up the pieces and drop them down her throat.

Lynsey was very happy. Only two things bothered her. One was that Maggie would fly away. Lynsey chose not to think about that one.

The other was that a cat would get her. The local cats used the garden as a road. Paul and Lynsey stuffed up all the holes in the thick green hedge. The fat furry tabby cat was the worst. He was so big that it seemed impossible for him to squeeze through the gaps in the hedge. Lynsey was sure he climbed over it to get into the garden.

So Lynsey never left Maggie on her own. If she went into the house she took the bird with her, even to the toilet. Everywhere Lynsey went, Maggie went. She needed watching all the time.

# Chapter Nine

Mum was on 'Maggie Watch'. It was a very hot day. She was sitting in a deck-chair reading. Maggie was sun-bathing, lying on the grass, with her wings stretched out like an aeroplane. Mum fell asleep in the sun.

Lynsey and Marie were playing upstairs. Suddenly there was a loud yell. Lynsey ran downstairs just in time to see Tabby go scuttling through the hedge. Mum was chasing Tabby and shouting her head off.

There was no sign of Maggie.

Mum had woken up and seen Tabby, like a small tiger, crouched ready to pounce on Maggie. The bird was still fast asleep. She had not seen, or heard or smelled the cat only inches away from her.

Tabby had gone but so had Maggie.

Lynsey called and called. No Maggie. She was crying.

'The cat didn't get her, Lynsey. I'm sure,' said Mum. 'Maggie is probably scared and hiding.'

At last they found her. She had crawled right inside a bush and kept very still. She only came out when Lynsey reached inside the broad leaves for her.

'You said you'd watch.' Lynsey thought it was Mum's fault.

'I know. I'm sorry. I must have dozed off for a few minutes.'

'But Tabby could have got her.'

'He could have, but he didn't. Remember we keep asking God to look after her. It is a good job he doesn't fall asleep in the sun!'

'Why did she go into the bush?' asked Marie.

'She just knew it was a safe place,' replied Mum. 'She is learning that cats are bad news.'

They all decided that Maggie must learn to fly to get out of trouble. So the flying lessons started again. Lynsey did not want Dad to do it. So she took Maggie down the garden.

'It's all right, little Maggie. It won't hurt. You've got to learn because of the cats.'

Lynsey copied what Dad had done. Maggie gently glided down onto the grass but that was all. This went on for a few days. Sometimes the bird would run away if she thought it was time for a flying lesson.

One day Paul was watching.

'It's no use having a bird that can only fly *down*,' he said. 'Here, give her to me. She's got to fly *up*.' And he threw Maggie into the air. It worked!

Her wings flapped and she went round in a circle before landing at their feet. Paul did it again and again. Then Maggie was tired and they gave her just one cherry as a reward.

There was no stopping her. At night she flew around the garage. They never knew where she would be in the morning. When Lynsey opened the garage door, the black and white shape would swoop across and land on her shoulder. Her claws were really strong now and dug into Lynsey's skin. Lynsey was always scared that Maggie would plop on her, but she never did.

Maggie was slowly learning to feed herself. She was not keen on the idea. It was much easier to let someone drop the bits of meat down her throat than to learn to do it herself. Lynsey put bits of mince on the ground so she would peck at them. She did not get a lot, so was still fed by hand sometimes.

She could drink water though. Maggie would stand on her dish and have a big drink. Then she would have a bath in it.

One day Paul and Lynsey filled a washing-up bowl with water. They put some twigs on top, so it was like a pond. Then they put Maggie

on the twigs. She tried to have a drink, fell off the twig and got soaked. She was really cross and sulked in the sun until she was dry.

Soon after this Lynsey could not find Maggie anywhere. Now that she could fly the family left her on her own in the garden. But today she was not in the garden. Not in a bush, not up the apple tree, not behind the shed, not anywhere. They all shouted her name.

'Maggie! Maggie!'

She swooped down the hill, across the gardens and landed on Dad's shoulder. He gave her a piece of meat. They all made a big fuss of her. She looked almost grown-up.

'She'll go soon,' said Dad. 'She will soon be back in the wild.'

More than ever Lynsey did not want her to go. She wanted her to stay with them for ever. Maggie could live in the garden, go off flying, but always come back to them.

Every time they went out, they left Maggie in the garden. As soon as Lynsey returned home she would run into the garden. It was always a relief to find Maggie. Sometimes she was up a tree, or hiding in her favourite bush. Sometimes she took her time to come home from one of the other gardens. But she always came back to Lynsey. Always, that is, until one awful day.

# Chapter Ten

It was a lovely day to begin with. It was warm again and they were all going to visit a craft fair. In one of the big parks there were lots of huge tents and marquees. Inside people were making and selling all sorts of things.

Lynsey loved the stall where the man was cutting patterns into wood. She queued for ages. Then she watched while the man wrote 'Lynsey' in big curly letters, and drew an outline of a magpie. The smell of the burnt wood mixed with the musty smell of the tent. Lynsey paid her money. She would put her name on her bedroom door.

They watched a potter making jars and vases. They were very nice, but cost lots of money.

'Paul, don't touch,' said Mum. 'If you break one of these it will cost a fortune.'

Paul wandered off to watch an artist painting a sea with wild pounding waves. People were making things out of glass, metal, dried flowers, and even bits of scrap iron. The family spent ages watching and bought a few gifts for birthdays. After stocking up on home-made fudge and real lemonade, Lynsey got restless. Maggie had been on her own for ages. She might be lonely.

As usual, Lynsey ran into the back garden calling for her bird. Nothing happened. She shouted and looked. Paul, Mum and Dad joined in the search. Nothing. No Maggie. No sign of her anywhere.

They all walked up the road calling for Maggie. The neighbours had not seen her. No-one had. It was no use. Maggie had gone.

'She's gone back to the wild,' said Dad, hugging Lynsey, who was crying. 'It had to happen.'

Even Mum was sad. She got a bowl and scrubbed the last blobs of plop off the garage floor.

Dad put Lynsey's nameplate on the bedroom door. The picture of the magpie made Lynsey cry even more.

'Remember, Lynsey,' he said, 'we prayed that God would look after Maggie. Well he has. Now she is free. She is where she belongs.'

'But I wanted her to stay.'

'I know, but it's best this way.'

Lynsey did not agree. Why could not God

have made Maggie stay at her house? She had not even said goodbye.

Every day Lynsey looked for Maggie. There was no sign of her. The fat cat, Tabby, seemed to have a smile between his whiskers. If he had had Maggie! . . . the thought was too awful.

Then a few days later the phone rang.

'Lynsey, it's Marie's mum,' called Mum, sounding very excited. 'Maggie is sitting in their front garden, picking heads off the flowers.'

Paul and Lynsey ran as fast as they could to Marie's house. It was true! It *was* Maggie. She ran to Lynsey who picked her up. Marie's mum gave them a chunk of cheese and they fed bits to Maggie.

'She looks thinner,' sighed Lynsey. 'She's not eating enough.'

'Don't worry,' Paul said. 'She was getting too fat anyway. Look, her feathers are shiny and strong.'

Maggie soared onto the roof and did not want to come down. Lynsey watched her until Mum came to see what was happening and to take them home. Maggie followed, hopping along the rooftops until they reached the top of their road. Then she flew away out of sight.

About a week later Marie came bursting in. 'You know my big sister? She says that Maggie lives at her school.'

'How does she know?' asked Lynsey.

'Well, there is a very tame magpie there. When they eat their sandwiches outside, it comes right up to them. My sister says it eats the bits of crisps and any other things that people don't want.'

'Are you sure?'

'Of course. I bet she pinches the best bits of food,' said Marie.

So Maggie was okay. There was enough food to feed a flock of birds at the big school.

Lynsey still loved Maggie very much. She would never forget her. Perhaps it was best that Maggie went off to live in the wild. God had looked after the bird while she lived at Lynsey's house. God would carry on looking after her.

Every time Lynsey sees a magpie in the garden or on the roof, she thinks it is Maggie.

'Please God, look after Maggie,' she says, as she watches the bird. All grown-up magpies look the same to Lynsey. She can never be sure if it is Maggie. But one of the amazing things about God is that he knows. He knows exactly which bird is Maggie. He knew she needed Lynsey to care for her until she was big and strong. And he knows that Maggie is still very important to Lynsey. That is why she believes he still looks after Maggie. Don't you think so, too?